The Trouble with the Johnsons

by MARK TEAGUE

SCHOLASTIC
HARDCOVER

SCHOLASTIC INC.

New York

IT was a warm, sunny morning
in the city, but Elmo Freem was unhappy.
He was homesick. Elmo had moved to the city
just the day before. His parents had moved,
too, of course, and so had his cat, Leon,
but still the boy felt sad. He wanted
to go back to his house in the country.

Leon missed the old house, too. He hid under Elmo's bed and came out only when he was hungry.

That afternoon Elmo's mother said that she wished he would give their new home a chance. "The city is a wonderful place," she said. "Why don't you go outside and have a look around?"

Elmo's mother was right. There were
many new things to see in the neighborhood.
For a while Elmo forgot to be unhappy.
But on his way home he came across a group
of children playing in the street. One boy
asked Elmo his name. Elmo told him.
The boy, whose name was Buford Snark,
laughed. "Elmo Freem!" he shouted.
"That's the stupidest name I ever heard."
While the other children laughed, Elmo crept
back to his apartment.

Late that night Elmo woke up
to find Leon clawing his shoulder.

"Come on," said the cat. "It's time
for us to go."

Elmo was surprised. Leon had never
spoken before. "Go where?" he asked.

"Home," said Leon. "Back
to the country."

The city seemed like a different place
that night. For one thing, the people were different.
They were not like people at all,
but reminded Elmo of the pictures
in his dinosaur book.
"There is something
very strange about this," he thought
as he followed Leon down the street.
Soon Elmo was quite lost. He didn't worry
though, since Leon was there. Elmo had
once heard that cats can always find
their way home.

Before long they arrived at a subway station. Elmo had never traveled on a subway train, but he followed Leon down the stairs, telling himself, "I'm sure it's perfectly safe."

A train entered the station. Elmo and Leon climbed aboard. The train sped through dark tunnels and weirdly lit caverns.

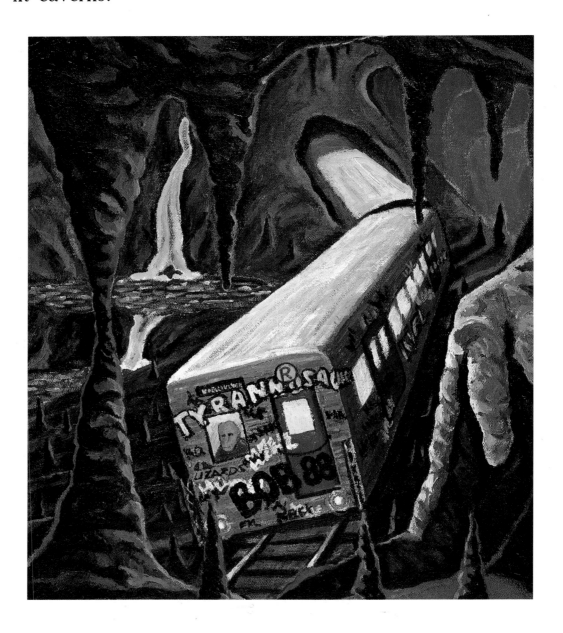

As the train ride continued, Elmo tried reading the advertisements on the train-car walls. He was never sure afterwards how long the train ride lasted. Perhaps he slept....

Finally, with a loud screech the train
came to a stop. Elmo and Leon stepped out
onto the platform and headed upstairs. It was
a sunny afternoon. They stood in the middle
of a large, grassy field. Across the field
was a road, and at the end of the road,
sitting atop a small hill, was their old house.

"Home at last," said Elmo Freem
as Leon trotted ahead.

When he reached his house Elmo found
a strange name on the mailbox.
Could a new family have moved in?
It hardly seemed possible.

Leon, who could not read, ran ahead
unconcerned. He jumped onto the porch
and clawed at the front door as he had
always done whenever he wished
to go inside.

When the door opened Leon hissed and dove behind Elmo. Elmo was also surprised by the large figure who stood in the doorway. Except for the dress and apron she wore, the figure looked very much like a dinosaur.

"Hello," she said. "I am Mrs. Johnson."

"Hello," Elmo stammered. "This used to be my house."

All that afternoon the boy and his cat
sat outside their old home. Elmo was afraid
to ask Mrs. Johnson if they could
come inside.

That evening Mr. Johnson drove up
in the family car.
He glanced at Elmo and Leon
but said nothing as he hurried inside.
"These Johnsons are very strange people,"
thought Elmo as he wondered what
to do next.

It was quite dark out when Mrs. Johnson
appeared on the front porch and asked them
if they would like to come in for dinner.

After dinner Elmo was given his old bedroom to sleep in. He told Leon how glad he was to be back home. Still, it was some time before either of them fell asleep.

For a while they enjoyed their life
with the Johnsons. Elmo played
on his tire swing and Leon hunted
squirrels in the woods behind
the house.

The Johnsons were very kind.
They treated Elmo as if he were
their own little boy and Leon as if
he were their cat. In fact, they treated
both pretty much the same.

Mrs. Johnson fed them every day,
and one night Mr. Johnson took them
all to the drive-in movie theater.

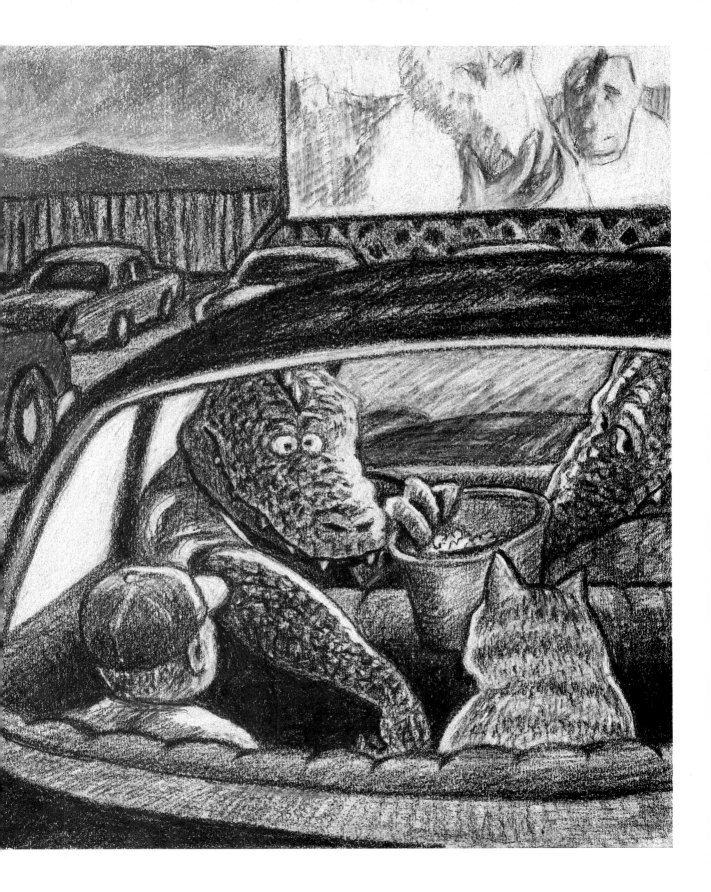

Privately, though, Elmo began to
be unhappy. He liked the Johnsons,
yet somehow they made him uncomfortable.
He began to miss his parents very much.

The house now seemed strange to him.
He didn't think of it as "home" anymore.

One day Elmo found Leon out
in the woods. The cat was leaning against
a tree while squirrels hopped around
in the branches above his head. Elmo told
Leon he was homesick. The cat nodded.
He was homesick, too.

"The Johnsons are nice people," said Elmo,
"but they aren't like Mom and Dad."

Leon nodded. "Let's face it," he said,
"they're really just giant lizards."

At dinner that night Elmo told the Johnsons that they wanted to go home.

"Oh, dear," said Mrs. Johnson.

"Come now, Trudy," said Mr. Johnson. "You knew it had to happen eventually."

"I suppose so," said Mrs. Johnson, "but it's been so nice having them around."

"Wait right there," said Mr. Johnson to Elmo. "I'll get the car keys."

Elmo dozed through most of the long ride home. He was half asleep when the Johnsons hugged him good-bye. "Be good," they said, and drove away.

Elmo was happy the next morning when he woke up in his bed in the new apartment. He was surprised that his parents said nothing about his having been away, but he didn't worry much about it. Leon never said anything about their adventure, either.

Soon Elmo and Leon came to think of the apartment as home. Cats don't change their habits overnight, but at least Leon didn't spend so much time under the bed. Elmo, on the other hand, played with the neighborhood children nearly every day. Before long Buford Snark became his best friend.

Elmo rarely thought about his old house...

... but sometimes, late at night,
the Johnsons called on the telephone,
merely, they told him, to say "hello."

For
Laura

Library of Congress Cataloging-in-Publication Data

Teague, Mark.
The trouble with the Johnsons / by Mark Teague.
p. cm.
Summary: Unhappy with their family's move to the city, Elmo and
his cat Leon take a nocturnal journey to their old house in the
country but find that things are somehow not the same there.

ISBN 0-590-42394-0

[1. Moving, Household--Fiction.   2. City and town life--Fiction.
3. Cats--Fiction.]   I. Title.
PZ7.T2193825Tr   1989
[E]--dc19   88-38532   CIP
                                               AC

12 11 10 9 8 7 6 5 4 3 2 1   9/8 0 1 2 3 4/9
Printed in Hong Kong   38
First Scholastic printing, September 1989